BASKET

A Richard Jackson Book

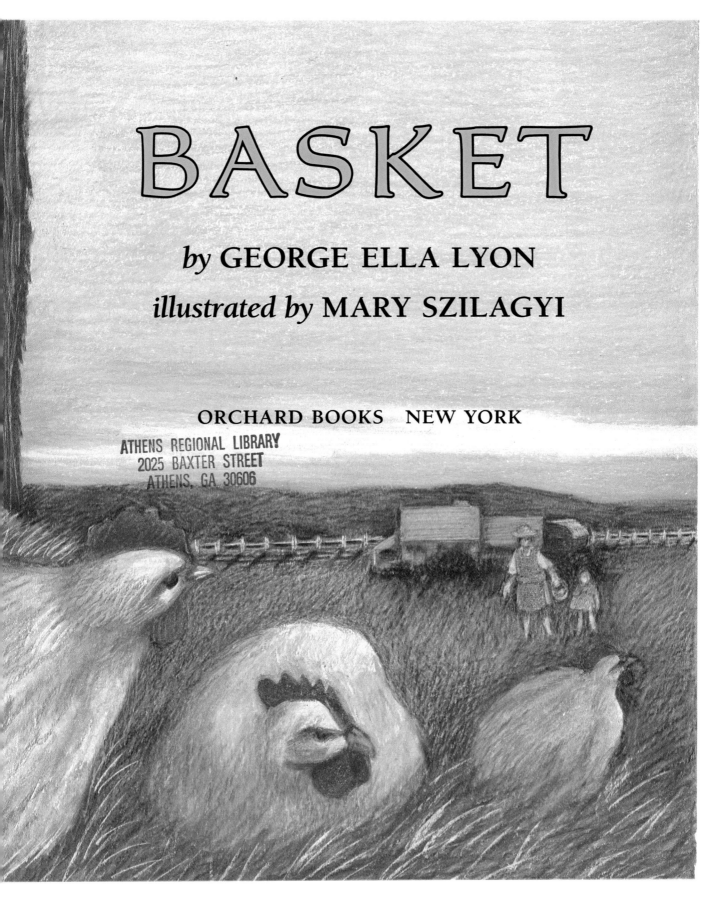

BASKET

by GEORGE ELLA LYON

illustrated by MARY SZILAGYI

ORCHARD BOOKS   NEW YORK

In memory of my grandmother
Ruby Lane Fowler

and for her newest great-grandchildren
Alex, Caitlin, Sadie, Joey, and Gant

G.E.L

To Dorothy K. Connor

M.S.

My grandmother had a little white oak basket, left from the farm, from years of keeping chickens, gathering eggs.

My mama says it was her kitchen basket when they
moved to town. It might have peaches in it,
pot holders, roses. Scissors in the bottom sometimes.

If Mama wanted to cut out paper dolls,
Grandmother would say, "Go look in
my little basket."

If Mama got hungry, Grandmother told her,
"The basket is full of ripe plums."

One Christmastime, Grandmother filled it with holly, forgetting the flashlight underneath.

Mama had to dig it out when the power went off.

Ow.

Grandmother moved before I was born to an
apartment above my daddy's store. She had her desk from
the old house, her big striped chair with the footstool,
her double-globe milk-glass lamp. But the basket
got lost in the move.

And everything she couldn't find was in it.

If she was sewing, she'd say, "I packed that little basket special, with all my best thread."

Or if we were sorting pictures for the album, "That basket had my picture stickers in it, my bottle of white ink."

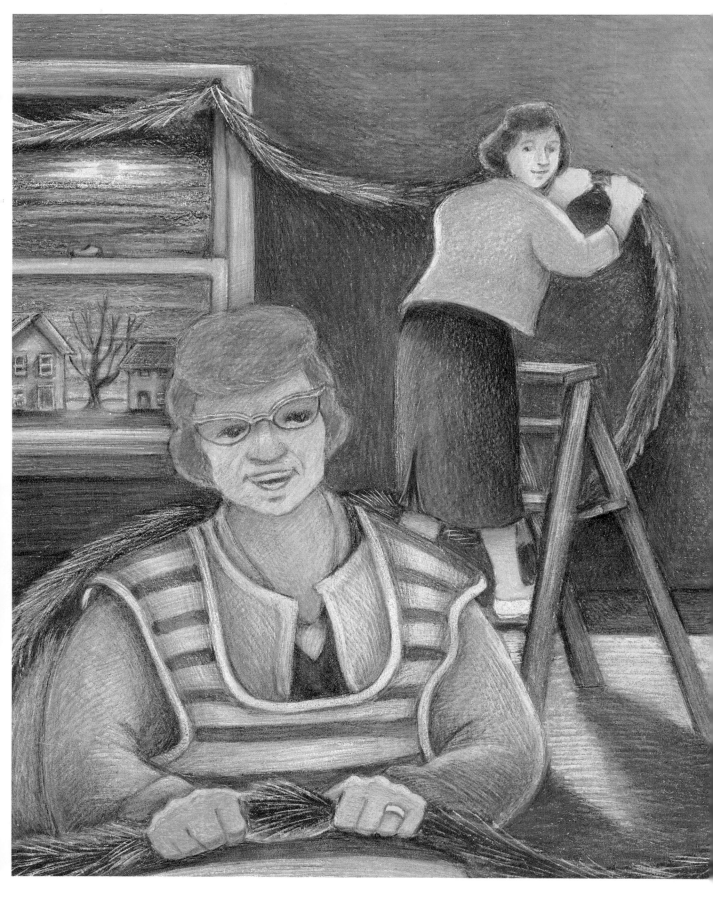

At Christmas she was sure the lost basket held her list of friends to send cards.

My mama laughed. "That basket gets bigger all the time."

Grandmother just sang:

> *Spool of thread*
> *Spool of thread*
> *Thimbleful of flour*
> *Will make my bread.*

Come spring, Mama couldn't find the small pick
Grandmother used to work her flower garden.
"I know," she said, smiling. "It's in the basket."
Grandmother looked stern. "I should have
never packed that basket," she told us. "I should
have carried it myself."

My grandmother lived a long time. When she died, we found in the closet in the cedar chest wrapped in tissue paper inside a pillowcase her little basket.

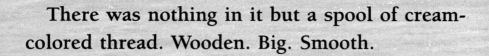

There was nothing in it but a spool of cream-colored thread. Wooden. Big. Smooth.

Spool of thread
Spool of thread
We'll all dine
On a darning egg.

Mama said I could have it. I still keep it in
the basket with stories of holly and peaches
and flashlights, with memories of feathers
and scissors and plums.

Spool of thread
Spool of thread
Stitch us together
And we won't go beg.

I draw out the thread and hear
my grandmother sing.